THE MAGIC IN A SMILE

Schiffer Publishing Ltd®

4880 Lower Valley Road • Atglen, PA 19310

Max hadn't started off the day at his best. Being used to his father's patience waking him up, today he found it would be his grandma who, all of a sudden, would turn on the lights, forcing him to wake up in fits and starts.

CLICK

In a bad mood, he rose and popped downstairs for breakfast, feeling kind of grumpy. At the table he came across his second disappointment: He wanted **to have cereal, which is his favorite, but there wasn't any left.** And so he had to eat a sandwich instead. Since he didn't like that sandwich at all, it took very long to finish it, and Grandma reacted by asking him if he was still a little baby. **He really hated it when people said that to him!**

At school, he was feeling a bit edgy and couldn't focus on the tasks he had to do. HE COULDN'T get anything right!

At lunchtime, while sitting in the school's cafeteria, Max found out that fish was on the menu. And how he hated that yucky fish . . . yuuuuuck!

It took him ages to finish the dish, and when he did, he barely had time to play. Max felt more angry and edgy as the day went by.

Finally, later that afternoon, **MAX'S ANGER EXPLODED** when Bertha took his toy from him. His head, which was his thinking machine, couldn't help it, and all the rage and anger that had been rising up during the day burst out at once.

Max grabbed Bertha's arm and bit it, leaving a mark on it . . .

That day the teacher **suspended him.**

When Mum and Dad came by to pick him up, they found out what had happened and **were very upset with him.**

3415
× 3
?
2110
375+
444
4×
2413
× 5
12066
345
+179
524
ZOOLOGIE.
ENTOMOLOGIE
Orthoptères.

Luckily, today was the day the **family was visiting his great-grandfather,** who had caught a cold. Max loved him so dearly and really enjoyed listening to his stories. He liked the way his great-grandfather treated him as a grown-up boy.

While Mum and Dad were distracted, his great-grandfather, who noticed even the tiniest detail, asked:

"What is it, Max? Did you have a bad day?"

"Yes. I think today was the **worst day of my life.**"

"Ah! I've had days like that myself. Can I ask you something?"

"Did you ever notice what happens **when somebody laughs?** Did you notice what happens to everyone who is around someone who's laughing?"

"**Hmm . . . I don't understand what you're trying to say . . .**"

Then, the grandfather **burst out laughing as if he'd just seen the funniest thing in the whole world,** and, soon after, Max couldn't help but join him in his laughter.

"**Laughter is contagious.** You understand it now?"

"It's true! Though I wasn't feeling like laughing at all, **you made me!**"

"Well, little friend . . . everybody can help in his or her own way. Did you know **every single smile is magical?**"

"How do you know all these things?"

"It is time that teaches you, Max. Also, I know when we are angry it works exactly the same way. Those around us notice it, and **things don't work out as nicely as they should when we feel edgy.**"

"Now that you've learned these little secrets,
would you like to start the day over?"

"I . . . Why not . . ." answered Max, a bit scared.

His great-grandpa drew some kind of powder
from his pocket, and blew it at the boy's face.
And right then, as if by magic . . .

His grandma woke him up in fits
and starts by turning the lights on
all of a sudden.

Still feeling a bit surprised, Max drew a smile on his face and **his grandma gave him an enormous kiss!** Feeling joyful, he rose from bed and popped downstairs for breakfast.

As his favorite cereal ran out, he gladly accepted the sandwich to eat instead. Grandma was so happy **she praised Max** and told him how **every day that went** by he **looked older and more mature.**

At school he finished his tasks soon, as he felt joyful and could focus easily on them, and **the teacher even rewarded him** for it. At lunchtime, he made a great effort eating that fish he didn't like and finished early. Everything was running smoothly . . .
great-grandpa had answers to everything!

That afternoon, when Bertha grabbed his toy, **he smiled brightly,** told her he was playing with that toy at the moment, and took it back. His teacher praised him in front of his classmates, and when Mum and Dad came to pick him up, **they were very happy with his attitude.**

As he knew well, that same afternoon they were visiting his great-grandfather, who had caught a cold

As soon as Max and his great-grandpa saw each other, they started laughing out loud, and soon Mum and Dad joined too. **The four of them were now laughing!**

While Mum and Dad were distracted, Max's great-grandpa whispered in his ear:

"So, how was your day?"

"You were right about everything, Grandpa.
There's magic in a smile!
It makes difficult things look simple!"

"You bet, little one!"

AAAA HAA HA

Beyond the Tale

In this tale we meet Max, a boy who finds in his great-grandfather the needed help in discovering how, in each situation, one can react in two opposite ways. The first kind of response can be described as more adaptive and consists of communication, willpower, smiling, etc. On the other hand, there is a more maladaptive kind of response, such as violence, passivity, uncontrolled anger, etc.

IN ORDER TO ACHIEVE HAPPINESS FOR OURSELVES AND THE ONES SURROUNDING US, IT IS VERY IMPORTANT THAT EACH ONE OF US — INCLUDING CHILDREN AND ADULTS — BECOMES RESPONSIBLE FOR HIS OR HER ACTIONS AND DECIDES WHICH PATH TO CHOOSE. WE CANNOT PREDICT WHAT WILL HAPPEN TO US, BUT WE CAN DECIDE HOW TO REACT IN EACH SITUATION.

This tale can prove to be a useful tool for creating a suitable backdrop in which to establish effective emotional communication with our little ones when these unexpected and diverse situations appear. Thus, we may little by little become more capable of studying, improving, and guiding our actions toward welfare. At the same time, we will be avoiding our own emotional environment getting polluted, as we'll be contributing to its improvement.

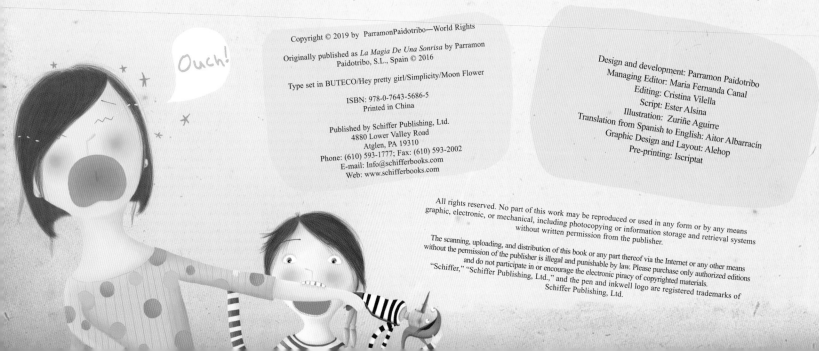

Ouch!

Design and development: Parramon Paidotribo
Managing Editor: Maria Fernanda Canal
Editing: Cristina Vilella
Script: Ester Alsina
Illustration: Zuriñe Aguirre
Translation from Spanish to English: Aitor Albarracín
Graphic Design and Layout: Alehop
Pre-printing: Iscriptat